This book belongs to:

D0537079

Blanca's Feather

Blanca's Feather

by **Antonio Hernández Madrigal**

illustrated by **Gerardo Suzán**

rising moon

To my sister, Sara, and her children, Paloma and Antonio Martin.

To Saint Francis of Assisi who loved all animals great and small, and to all his present followers.

—A. H. M.

The text type was set in Giovanni
The display type was set in Cafe Mimi
Composed in the United States of America
Edited by Aimee Jackson
Designed by Jennifer Schaber
Production supervised by Lisa Brownfield

Printed in Hong Kong by Midas Printing Company, Ltd.

FIRST IMPRESSION
ISBN 0-87358-743-x

Library of Congress Catalog Card Number 99–26017

Madrigal, Antonio Hernández.
  Blanca's feather / by Antonio Hernández Madrigal ; illustrated by
Gerardo Suzán.
    p. cm.
  Summary: When Rosalía can't find her hen Blanca in time for the
annual blessing of the animals on the Feast of St. Francis, she
finds a way around the problem and receives a surprise besides.
  ISBN 0-87358-743-X
  [1. Benediction Fiction. 2. Chickens Fiction. 3. Christian life
Fiction.] I. Suzán, Gerardo, 1962– ill. II. Title.
PZ7.M26575B1 2000
[E]—dc21   99–26017

26/7.5M/04-00

Author's Note

Every year on October fourth, Saint Francis of Assisi's Day, the blessing of the animals is celebrated in Mexico and many other countries, including the United States. Men, women, and children parade to the local church bringing their newborn farm animals and pets decorated with garlands of fresh flowers.

This traditional blessing of the animals dates back to the twelfth century. It is believed to have been inspired by Saint Francis of Assisi, who cared for and loved all animals as brothers and sisters, whether they were domestic, wild, large, or small. According to the belief, the blessing will protect the animals from disease and predators.

osalía rushed to the barn as the sun sank behind the mountain. She tossed a handful of corn in the air for her hen, Blanca. While Blanca ate the kernels of corn one by one, Rosalía began to think about the next day, the Day of Saint Francis of Assisi. Everyone in the valley was planning to take their farm animals and pets to the chapel for the yearly blessing. Rosalía couldn't wait to take Blanca to the chapel. The blessing would protect Blanca from the spirits of disease and from falling prey to coyotes and wolves.

As she fell asleep that night, Rosalía pictured herself in her favorite dress, holding Blanca in her arms.

Early the next morning, Rosalía hurried home from the market with a basket of flowers. Glancing at the clock on the kitchen wall, she began to help Mamá make garlands for the animals.

Meanwhile, her brothers prepared their own pets for the blessing. Juan brushed Chico, his pony. Roberto bathed Perla, a baby lamb.

As Mamá began to pat dough into round tortillas she said, "Rosalía, you'd better get dressed. Aren't you taking your hen to the blessing?"

"*Sí*, Mamá!" she exclaimed.

Rosalía dashed to her room and changed into her special dress. She braided pink ribbons into her hair, then ran to the barn to get her hen. "Blanca?" she called.

"*Mmm-oo-ooo*," Pinta, the cow, answered. But there was no answer from Blanca.

Rosalía searched in the stable. She peeked under the gate and called again, "Blanca, where are you?"

"*Neeeiiigh*," whinnied Marimba, the old mare.

But Blanca was nowhere in sight.

Rosalía ran outside. "Blanca! Blanca! Where are you?" she shouted across the garden of squash and beans.

Mamá stepped out of the farmhouse. "What's the matter?" she asked.

"I can't find Blanca!" Rosalía cried.

"She's been hiding lately," Mamá said. "Let's find her before it gets too late."

Rosalía and her mamá searched above the rafters in the barn and around the farmhouse. They peered over the tile roofs and even beyond the windmill.

As the sun got closer to the mountain peak, Juan said, "It's almost five o'clock, Rosalía. We will be late for the blessing."

"I don't think you will find Blanca in time," Roberto said. "We have to leave right now."

Rosalía's heart began to pound faster. "Then Blanca will be left without a blessing," she said.

"I am afraid so," Mamá said. "We'll just have to wait until next year."

As her brothers hurried to the chapel with their pets, Rosalía followed Mamá back to the farmhouse.

Without the blessing, Blanca will be unprotected for a whole year, Rosalía thought sadly. Anything could happen—Blanca might become ill or fall prey to hungry predators.

Suddenly, Rosalía spotted something white on a patch of straw. "Look Mamá!" she exclaimed. "It's one of Blanca's feathers!"

"Lately she's been losing feathers," Mamá said.

Then Rosalía got an idea. She picked up the feather. "Will Padre Santiago bless Blanca's feather?" she asked.

"Maybe he will. But you'd better hurry before the blessing is over," Mamá said.

Rosalía ran down the dirt road holding Blanca's feather. On the way she saw people already returning from the blessing with their animals wearing colorful garlands.

Señor Gregorio rode by on his horse, holding a baby goat in his arms. Señor Arturo and his son herded their piglet and cow. Others led calves or colts by a rope or carried puppies and kittens in their arms.

Rosalía finally caught up to her brothers. "Did you find Blanca?" Juan asked.

"No," Rosalía said. "But I'm bringing one of her feathers to the blessing."

"A feather?" Juan and Roberto laughed.

Rosalía stopped in the middle of the road. She felt angry and sad at the same time. She felt like turning back, but remembered the danger Blanca would be in for a whole year. Instead, she hid the feather in her pocket just in case the others might also make fun of her and she kept walking.

On their way to the chapel, Rosalía thought about Padre Santiago in his long, black robe. Would he laugh at her too and refuse to bless Blanca's feather?

When they arrived at the chapel in the main plaza, Rosalía saw that there were a few people still waiting in line. She was glad they hadn't missed the blessing after all.

Ahead of her, Señora Andrea held three kittens that crawled over her arms and shoulders. Looking down at Rosalía, Señora Andrea asked, "What did you bring to the blessing?"

"I brought a feather from my hen," Rosalía whispered.

"Just a feather?" Señora Andrea exclaimed.

"How silly to bring a feather to the blessing," giggled a girl as she stroked her dove, Chiquita.

"I'm sure Padre Santiago won't waste his time with a feather," snickered a boy carrying his parrot, Pancho.

Rosalía waited anxiously. When her turn finally came, she walked up to Padre Santiago.

Padre Santiago stared at Rosalía's empty arms. Bending down he asked, "What shall I bless for you this year, young lady?"

Rosalía could hear giggling behind her. Blushing, she pulled the feather out of her pocket and whispered, "I couldn't find my hen. I only brought one of her feathers."

"A feather?" Padre Santiago asked and paused for a moment. Rosalía held her breath as she watched Padre Santiago stroke his chin. Suddenly he smiled. "That was a good idea," he said. "At least I can bless one of her feathers."

Rosalía's face brightened. "Thank you, Padre," she said with a big grin as she handed the padre Blanca's feather.

While the others looked on, Padre Santiago reached into the bowl of holy water. Then, he carefully sprinkled the holy water on the feather. "When you find your hen, make sure to rub the feather on her head," he instructed Rosalía while handing her Blanca's feather.

Holding the precious feather, Rosalía followed her brothers home. As darkness began to fall over the mountains, she heard a coyote howling in the distance. Rosalía trembled. Had Blanca fallen prey to a hungry coyote?

It was almost dark when Rosalía and her brothers got home. Dashing into the kitchen she asked, "Mamá, have you seen Blanca?"

"No *mi'ja*," Mamá said softly.

"I'll never see Blanca again," Rosalía muttered. Sadly, she dragged herself across the patio. As she walked by the old clay oven, she suddenly heard the flapping of wings. Her heart began to pound. "Blanca?" she called, searching all around her.

Then Rosalía heard a familiar sound. *"Cluck, cluck,"* Blanca cackled as she sprang from the mouth of the oven.

"Oh, Blanca! You're safe!" Rosalía exclaimed with tears of joy streaming down her face. And to her great surprise, like a bouncing ball of feathers, a baby chick appeared behind Blanca. Then, one after another, a string of fluffy chicks sprouted from the hidden nest. *"Peep, peep,"* they twittered as they flapped their tiny wings around Blanca.

Rosalía dried her tears with the back of one hand. Remembering Padre Santiago's words, she pulled the feather out of her pocket. As the stars began to twinkle in the sky, Rosalía rubbed the feather on Blanca's head. Then she also rubbed the feather on each of Blanca's chicks.

That night as she snuggled into bed, Rosalía sighed with relief knowing that Blanca and her hatchlings were at last protected.

About the Author

ANTONIO HERNÁNDEZ MADRIGAL was born and raised, the sixth of ten children, in a small village in the state of Michoacán, Mexico. He immigrated to the United States in 1976, learning to read and write English while he worked as a harvester in the fields of southern Arizona. Eventually, Antonio began traveling and working throughout the United States, finally settling in San Diego where he began to live out his dream of becoming a writer.

Antonio is the author of: *The Eagle and the Rainbow: Timeless Tales from Mexico* (Fulcrum 1997) and *Erandi's Braids* (Putnam 1999), both illustrated by Tomie dePaola. Antonio currently lives in Carlsbad, California where he spends time in the local schools working with children, particularly those of migrant and other minority groups.

About the Illustrator

GERARDO SUZÁN, a national treasure of Mexico, has illustrated over fifty picture and juvenile books that have been published worldwide. He has participated in over sixty collective expositions in Mexico, the United States, Yugoslavia, Czech Republic, and Slovakia, and he has won many international awards. Gerardo says he likes working on picture books for children because he enjoys creating scenes that connect with reality, but at the same time portray a whimsical element of fantasy. Gerardo lives in the state of Coahuila, Mexico.

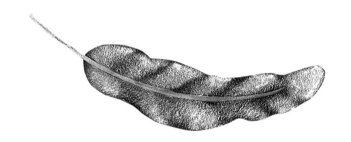